The Story of Wali Dâd

RETOLD AND ILLUSTRATED BY

KRISTINA RODANAS

LOTHROP, LEE & SHEPARD BOOKS   NEW YORK

The Story of Wali Dâd is based on "Wali Dâd, the Simple-hearted," retold by Andrew Lang in his *Brown Fairy Book* (1904). In trying to let the charm of this tale speak to today's readers, I have taken the liberty of substituting an act of human generosity for the fairy transformation in Lang's version. It seems to me more plausible—and equally magical.

K. R.

First Edition   1 2 3 4 5 6 7 8 9 10

Library of Congress Cataloging in Publication Data
Rodanas, Kristina. The story of Wali Dâd.
Summary: The desire of a poor, old grasscutter in India to share what little he has with a kind and beautiful woman begins an incredible chain of events. [1. India—Fiction] I. Title. PZ7.R5984St 1988   [E]   86-34423
ISBN 0-688-07262-3   ISBN 0-688-07263-1 (lib. bdg.)

For my mother and father, with love

Long ago in India there was an old man known as Wali Dâd. He lived all alone in a small mud hut at the edge of the jungle and made his living by cutting grass and selling it as horse feed. Although he earned little, Wali Dâd was very happy. Since his needs were few, he even managed to save several pennies a day, which he hid in a large clay crock.

One evening, after a particularly profitable day, the grasscutter saw that the clay crock was overflowing with coins.

It was time to spend his money.

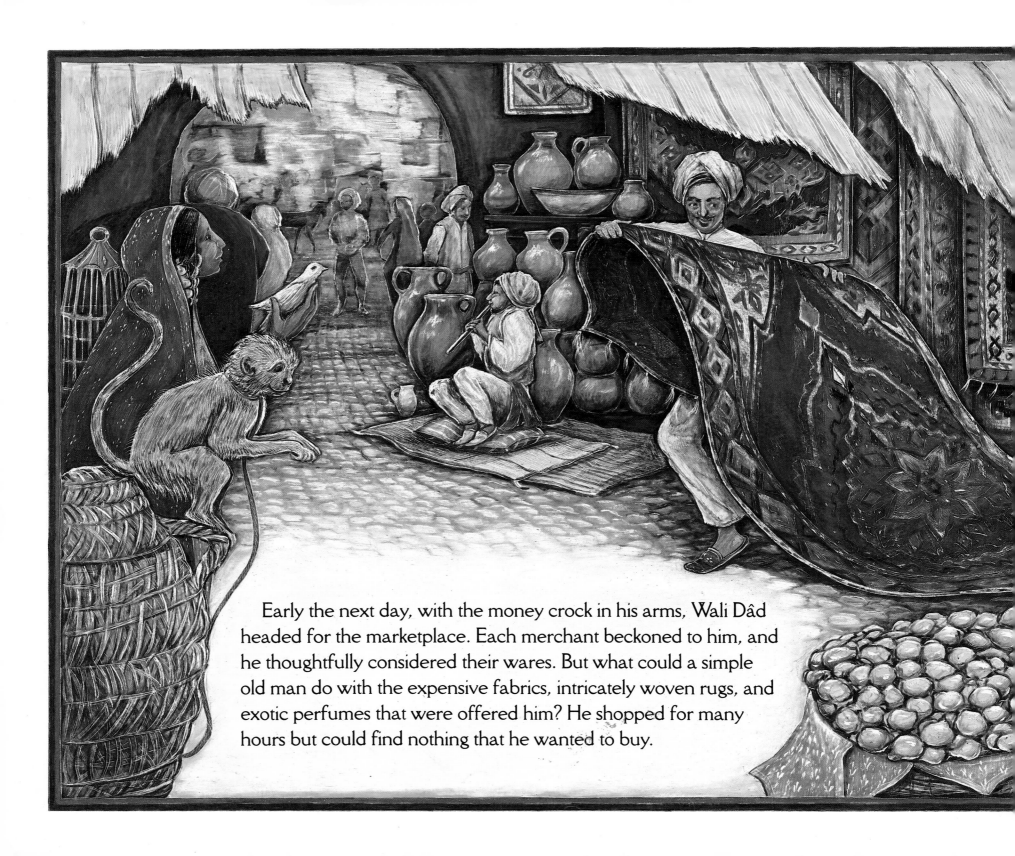

Early the next day, with the money crock in his arms, Wali Dâd
headed for the marketplace. Each merchant beckoned to him, and
he thoughtfully considered their wares. But what could a simple
old man do with the expensive fabrics, intricately woven rugs, and
exotic perfumes that were offered him? He shopped for many
hours but could find nothing that he wanted to buy.

Finally, Wali Dâd came to the last stall in the marketplace, a jewelry shop. A plain little bracelet caught his eye. Its smooth gold surface glowed in the afternoon light and invited him to take a closer look. He turned the bracelet over and discovered a beautiful pearl, carefully inlaid at the center. He purchased the bracelet at once and happily returned home.

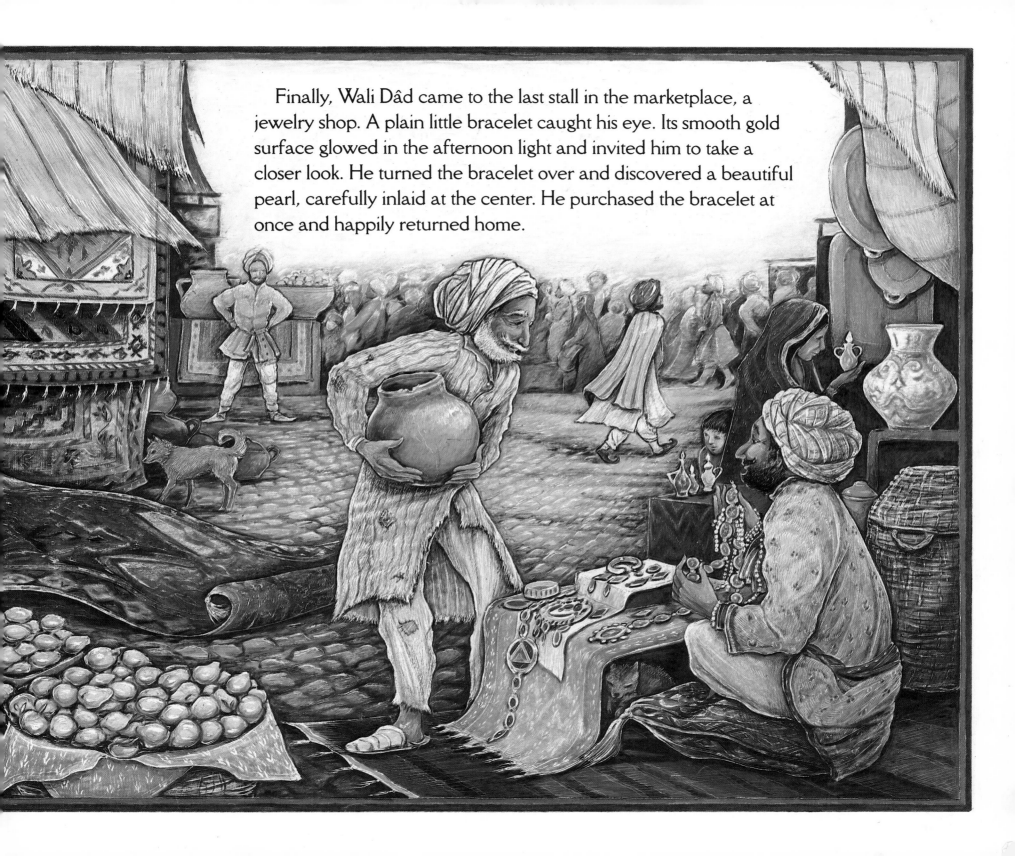

Wali Dâd soon realized the little bracelet was too wonderful to hide away in his mud hut. He wanted to share his treasure. So he went to the house of a traveling merchant who was his dear friend, and asked for the name of the kindest and most beautiful woman he had ever met.

The merchant had visited many different countries, so he had to think for a long time. "The Princess of Khaistan," he replied at last, "is by far the most beautiful, for she is known by all to be the most kind."

"Very well, then," said Wali Dâd, handing over the bracelet. "I would like you to give her this."

Much amused, his merchant friend agreed to deliver the gift on his next journey.

Months later, the merchant passed through Khaistan and presented the little bracelet to the Princess. She was delighted. To show her gratitude to the mysterious giver, she sent the merchant back with a return present, a camel-load of fine silks.

As requested, the merchant delivered the silks to Wali Dâd's mud hut. The old man was stunned, and could not imagine what to do with so precious a gift. Again he asked his friend for a name —the name of the most honorable young prince in all the land.

As before, the merchant thought and thought. "Well," he finally concluded, "the Prince of Nekabad is certainly the most honorable."

"Excellent," said Wali Dâd. "Would you please take these silks to him? I am sure he will find a fitting use for them."

The merchant promised to visit the Prince when he next traveled to Nekabad.

True to his word, the merchant journeyed to the royal palace of Nekabad, where he delivered the camel-load of silks. Indeed, the young Prince was most grateful. To repay the favor, he chose from his stable twelve splendid horses and told the merchant to take them to the very generous Wali Dâd.

The old grasscutter was astonished when the spirited horses pranced into his yard. "I have no stable, and I could never cut enough grass to feed them!" he cried.

He gave two horses to the merchant and persuaded his friend to take the remaining ten to the Princess of Khaistan.

Time passed, and when he next traveled to Khaistan, the merchant presented the Princess with the beautiful horses. Although she was very pleased, this time the Princess was somewhat perplexed. Such horses, she presumed, could only have come from the stables of a rich and powerful man. What courtesy might she return to one so wealthy?

The Princess asked her father, the King, for advice. Together they decided on a return present which they hoped the unknown giver would not feel obliged to repay. For each of the ten horses, the Princess requested that ten mules loaded with silver be sent to Wali Dâd.

The merchant led the procession.

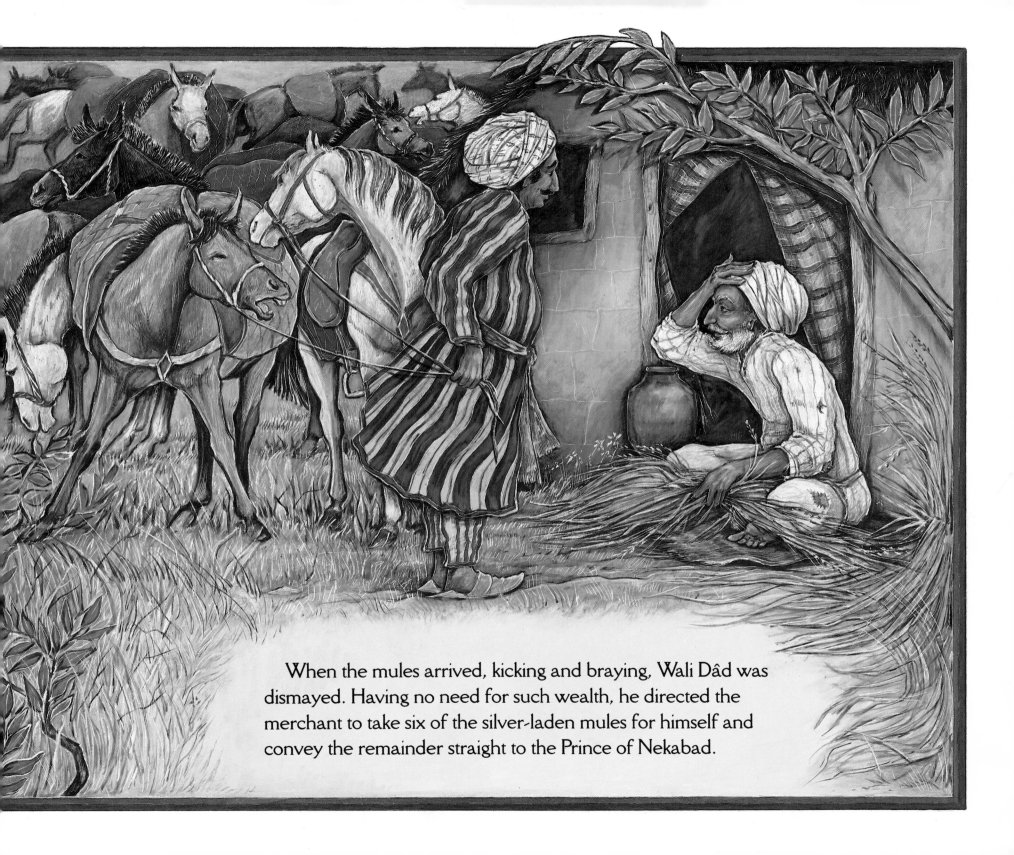

When the mules arrived, kicking and braying, Wali Dâd was dismayed. Having no need for such wealth, he directed the merchant to take six of the silver-laden mules for himself and convey the remainder straight to the Prince of Nekabad.

The Prince this time was more embarrassed than grateful. Such presents, he thought, must certainly be taxing the resources of the generous stranger. Hoping to put an end to this exchange of opulent gifts, he ordered up a herd of twenty each of his swiftest camels, his most magnificent horses, and his strongest elephants, all decorated in the finest of silks, leathers, and jewels.

With the help of a small troop of men, the merchant hastened the caravan to Wali Dâd's door...

...and the horrified Wali Dâd waved them on to the Princess of Khaistan, insisting that his friend keep two camels, two horses, and two elephants for his trouble.

You can well imagine the excitement at the gates of Khaistan when this incredible parade appeared. "What is the meaning of such generosity?" wondered the Princess.

The King thought he knew. "Of course," he said, "the great and princely Wali Dâd would like to meet you. Perhaps he is trying to win your hand in marriage. We must pay him a visit!"

The Princess agreed that they should visit Wali Dâd at once. A giant caravan was formed, complete with mounted soldiers, trumpets and flags, royal servants, magnificent chests of gold, bejeweled horses, camels, and elephants—and the King and Princess of Khaistan.

Reluctantly the merchant guided the procession toward the home of Wali Dâd.

The caravan moved slowly. As they came closer to their destination, the merchant grew increasingly nervous. If only he had revealed the simple truth about his friend!

When he reached Wali Dâd's mud hut, the merchant found his friend seated on a straw mat, munching his evening meal of dry bread and onions.

Wali Dâd gasped when he heard the merchant's news. "My house is far too small to receive all those guests," he cried, "and I haven't enough food to share with them! What am I to do?"

The merchant felt responsible for the situation, and he desperately wanted to help. "My dear friend," he said, "I have many servants and more than enough food to feed a caravan. Allow me to take care of the preparations. We will have a glorious reception for the King and Princess of Khaistan."

Wali Dâd gratefully accepted the merchant's offer.

That evening, with the help of his loyal servants, the merchant began to prepare for the royal guests. Wali Dâd had little to do but watch while servants trimmed the jungle grass surrounding his hut into a large courtyard. Exhausted, he fell asleep.

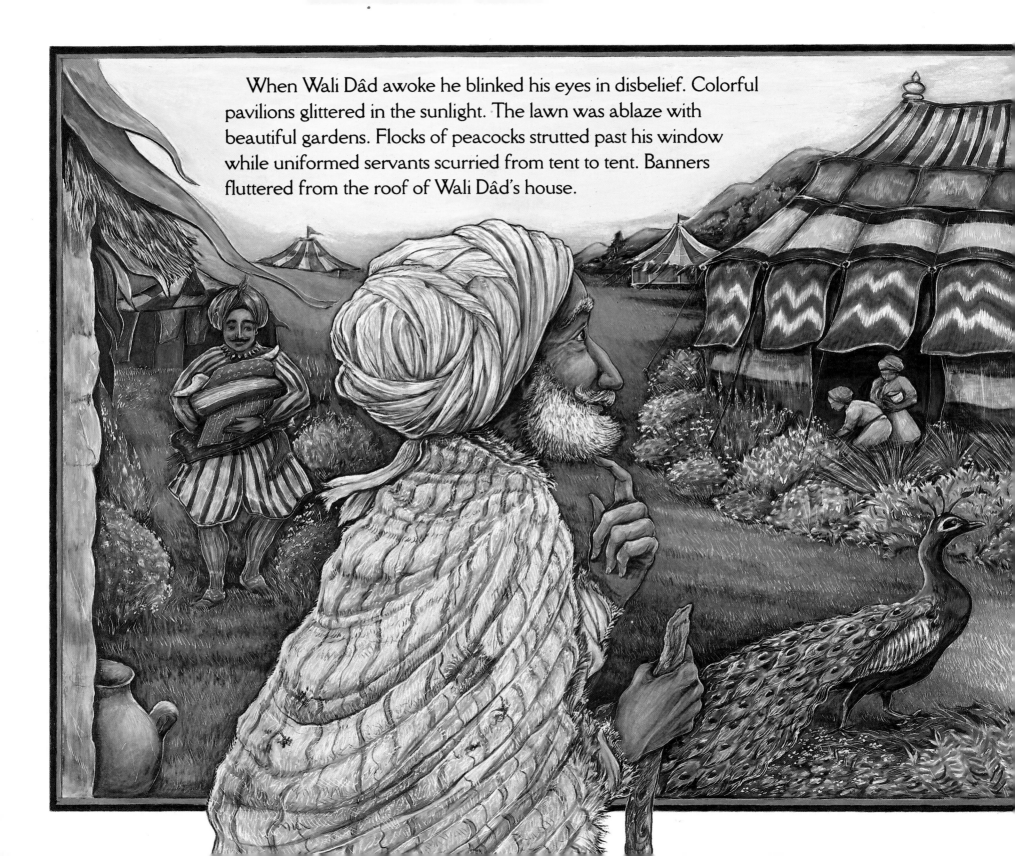

When Wali Dâd awoke he blinked his eyes in disbelief. Colorful pavilions glittered in the sunlight. The lawn was ablaze with beautiful gardens. Flocks of peacocks strutted past his window while uniformed servants scurried from tent to tent. Banners fluttered from the roof of Wali Dâd's house.

The merchant, looking tired but relieved, appeared in the doorway and presented Wali Dâd with a bundle of embroidererd clothing. "All is ready!" he announced proudly.

Amazed, Wali Dâd sent the merchant back with his humble invitation to the King and Princess of Khaistan.

The royal caravan arrived with a roaring of trumpets. Wali Dâd, clothed in silks and jeweled turban, welcomed his guests into the courtyard, where a tremendous feast was about to be served.

The King of Khaistan was most impressed and thanked his host for the generous reception. Then he took Wali Dâd aside and asked, "Is it true that you wish to marry my daughter?"

Wali Dâd was shocked by the question. He tried to think of a way to thank the King for the honor. "I am much too old and far too ugly to think of marrying the beautiful Princess," he replied at last. "But permit me to send for a loyal young friend who is far more worthy of winning your daughter's hand—the honorable Prince of Nekabad!"

The merchant departed for Nekabad and quickly returned with the Prince. At first glance he fell in love with the Princess and she with him.

There, that very day, the two were married. In their honor a splendid wedding feast was held which went on for three days and nights. Everyone celebrated their happiness.

But happiest of all was Wali Dâd. He had recognized the little gold bracelet proudly worn by the beautiful Princess of Khaistan.